SAN FRANCISCO
49ERS

SportsZone

BY MATT SCHEFF

abdopublishing.com

Published by Abdo Publishing, a division of ABDO, PO Box 398166, Minneapolis, Minnesota 55439. Copyright © 2017 by Abdo Consulting Group, Inc. International copyrights reserved in all countries. No part of this book may be reproduced in any form without written permission from the publisher. SportsZone™ is a trademark and logo of Abdo Publishing.

Printed in the United States of America, North Mankato, Minnesota
042016
092016

Cover Photo: Ric Tapia/AP Images
Interior Photos: Ric Tapia/AP Images, 1; AP Images, 4-5, 17; Bettmann/Corbis, 6-7, 8-9, 18-19; Harold Filan/AP Images, 10-11; Bob Campbell/San Francisco Chronicle/Corbis, 12; NFL Photos/AP Images, 13; Al Messerschmidt/AP Images, 14-15; Al Golub/AP Images, 16; Greg Trott/AP Images, 20-21; Susan Walsh/AP Images, 22-23; Marcio Jose Sanchez/AP Images, 24-25; Tony Avelar/AP Images, 26-27; Jeff Chiu/AP Images, 28-29

Editor: Todd Kortemeier
Series Designer: Nikki Farinella

Cataloging-in-Publication Data
Names: Scheff, Matt, author.
Title: San Francisco 49ers / by Matt Scheff.
Description: Minneapolis, MN : Abdo Publishing, [2017] | Series: NFL up close | Includes index.
Identifiers: LCCN 2015960450 | ISBN 9781680782325 (lib. bdg.) | ISBN 9781680776430 (ebook)
Subjects: LCSH: San Francisco 49ers (Football team)--History--Juvenile literature. | National Football League--Juvenile literature. | Football--Juvenile literature. | Professional sports--Juvenile literature. | Football teams-- California--Juvenile literature.
Classification: DDC 796.332--dc23
LC record available at http://lccn.loc.gov/2015960450

TABLE OF CONTENTS

THE CATCH

The fans at Candlestick Park were on their feet. Their San Francisco 49ers had the ball late in the fourth quarter of the 1981 National Football Conference (NFC) Championship Game. They trailed 27-21. Young quarterback Joe Montana stood at his 11-yard line. He looked out at the Dallas Cowboys' defense. It all came down to this drive. The winner was headed to the Super Bowl.

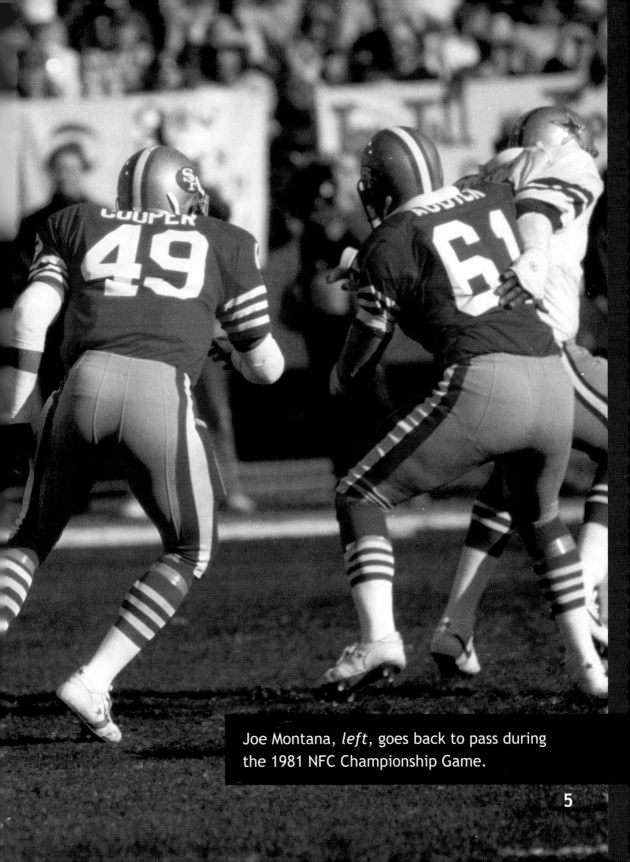

Joe Montana, *left*, goes back to pass during the 1981 NFC Championship Game.

FAST FACT

Dwight Clark's touchdown remains one of the most famous plays in National Football League (NFL) history. Fans know it simply as "The Catch."

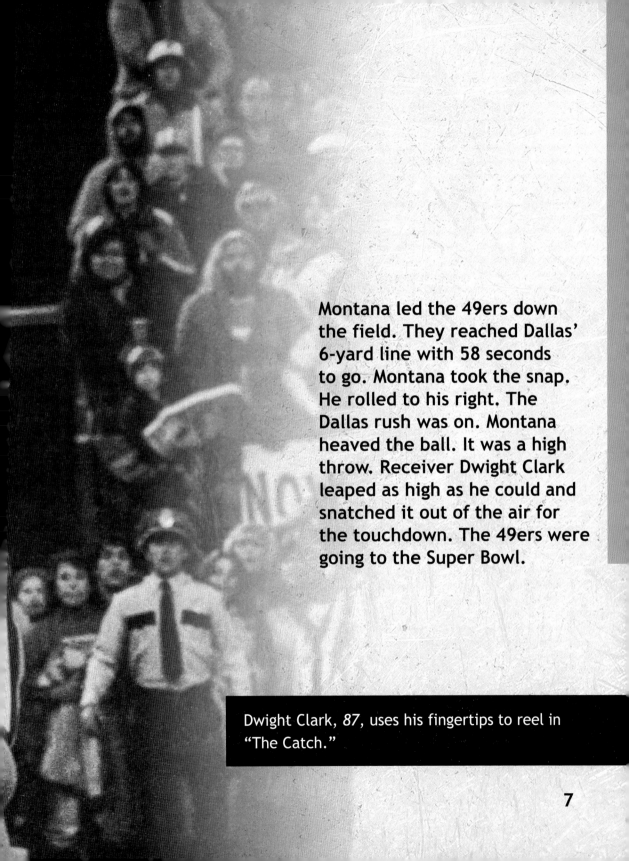

Montana led the 49ers down the field. They reached Dallas' 6-yard line with 58 seconds to go. Montana took the snap. He rolled to his right. The Dallas rush was on. Montana heaved the ball. It was a high throw. Receiver Dwight Clark leaped as high as he could and snatched it out of the air for the touchdown. The 49ers were going to the Super Bowl.

Dwight Clark, *87*, uses his fingertips to reel in "The Catch."

Buck Shaw, *right*, was the first coach in 49ers history.

BEGINNINGS

The 49ers started in 1946. San Francisco businessman Tony Morabito failed in his quest to get an NFL team. So he started a team playing in the newly formed All-America Football Conference (AAFC). The team was named for the 1849 gold rush, when people flocked to California looking to strike gold.

The 49ers were one of the AAFC's top teams. They went to the league's title game in 1949. But they lost to the Cleveland Browns.

FAST FACT

Y.A. Tittle was named the NFL Most Valuable Player (MVP) in 1957.

The AAFC folded after the 1949 season. All but three of its teams disbanded. The 49ers, Browns, and Baltimore Colts joined the NFL. The 49ers struggled at first. They went just 3-9 in 1950. But coach Buck Shaw turned things around. In 1951, the team drafted quarterback Y. A. Tittle. The prolific passer helped make the 49ers a better team.

San Francisco quarterback Y.A. Tittle, *14*, was inducted into the Pro Football Hall of Fame in 1971.

THE LEAN YEARS

The 49ers won plenty of games. Yet stars such as Y. A. Tittle and running back J. D. Smith could not bring playoff glory. The 49ers reached the playoffs just once in their first 20 NFL seasons. They did not win a single playoff game. In 1968, the team hired coach Dick Nolan. Nolan's defensive style helped the team turn things around.

FAST FACT

In 2005, the 49ers hired Dick Nolan's son, Mike Nolan, as head coach.

The 49ers made their first NFL playoff appearance in 1957 but lost to the Detroit Lions 31-27.

Abe Woodson was a standout player on defense and kick returns for the 49ers in the 1960s.

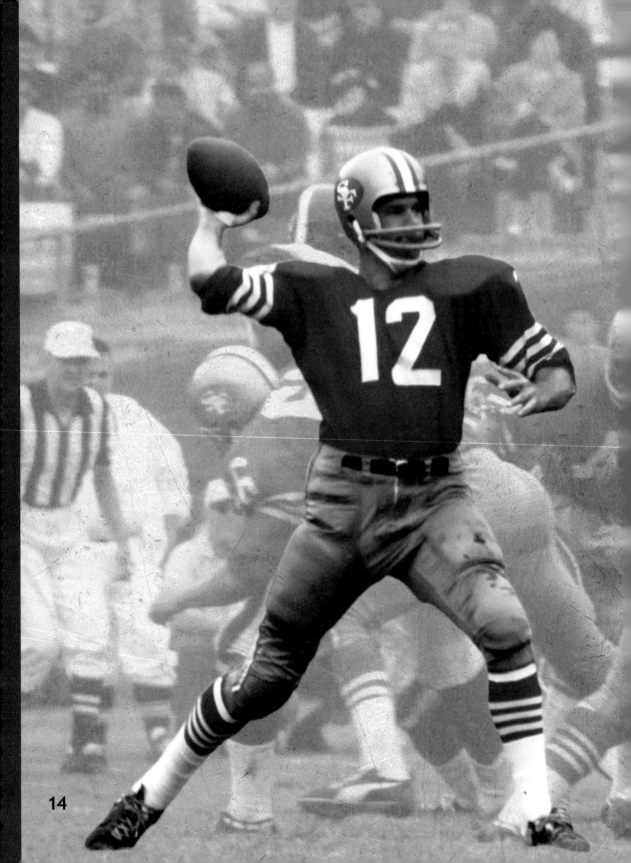

FAST FACT

The 49ers moved from Kezar Stadium to Candlestick Park in 1971. It remained their home through the 2013 season.

Nolan and quarterback John Brodie led the 49ers to three straight NFC West division titles from 1970 to 1972. However, the Dallas Cowboys stood in their way. Dallas knocked San Francisco out of the 1970 and 1971 playoffs. The 49ers looked like they would finally break through in the 1972 playoffs. They led 28-13 in the fourth quarter. But Dallas came back to win and end the 49ers' season again.

Quarterback John Brodie, *12*, led the 49ers to three straight division titles.

DYNASTY

By the late 1970s, the 49ers were one of the NFL's worst teams. But change was coming. The team hired coach Bill Walsh in 1979. It also drafted quarterback Joe Montana. Montana was the perfect fit for Walsh's new style of offense. The "West Coast" offense focused on short passes. In 1981, with the help of "The Catch," the 49ers beat the Cowboys in the NFC Championship.

Bill Walsh's West Coast offense turned the 49ers' franchise around.

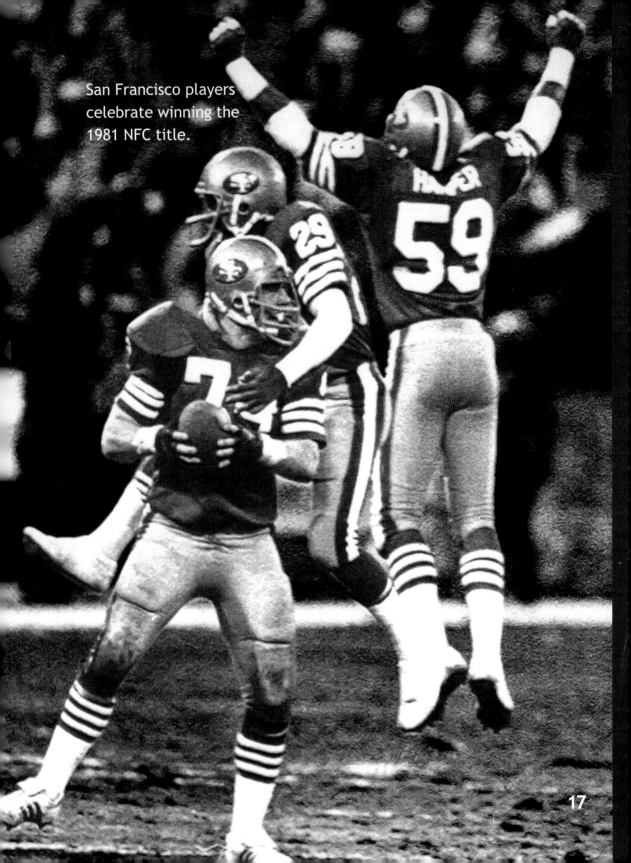

San Francisco players celebrate winning the 1981 NFC title.

The 49ers faced the Cincinnati Bengals in the Super Bowl. Montana won MVP of the game in leading the 49ers to a 26-21 victory. On the other side of the ball, hard-hitting defensive back Ronnie Lott led one of the league's best defenses. It was the start of a dynasty. The 49ers forced teams into making mistakes and gave up very few points. The 1984 season may have been the best in 49ers history. They went 15-1 and beat the Miami Dolphins for their second Super Bowl title.

FAST FACT

Joe Montana is one of three NFL quarterbacks to win four Super Bowls. The others are Terry Bradshaw and Tom Brady.

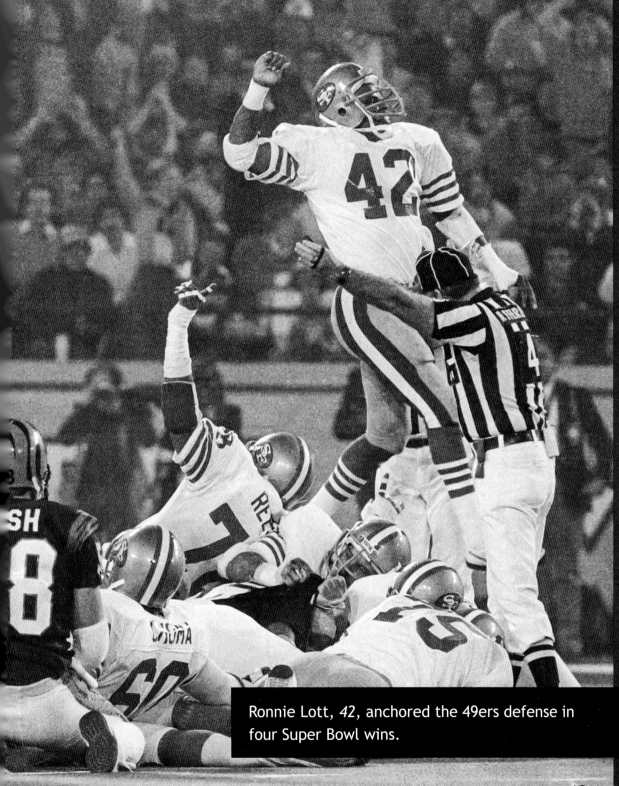

Ronnie Lott, 42, anchored the 49ers defense in four Super Bowl wins.

FAST FACT

Bill Walsh retired after the 1988 season. George Seifert took over as coach.

The 49ers added a new weapon for Montana in the 1985 draft in wide receiver Jerry Rice. The already powerful offense got even better. The 49ers won back-to-back Super Bowls in 1988 and 1989. They seemed poised to add another in 1990. But after a 14-2 season, San Francisco lost in the NFC title game.

Joe Montana, *16*, and Jerry Rice, *80*, dominated the NFL in the 1980s and 1990s.

FAST FACT

Hall of famer Jerry Rice is the NFL's all-time leader in catches, yards, and receiving touchdowns.

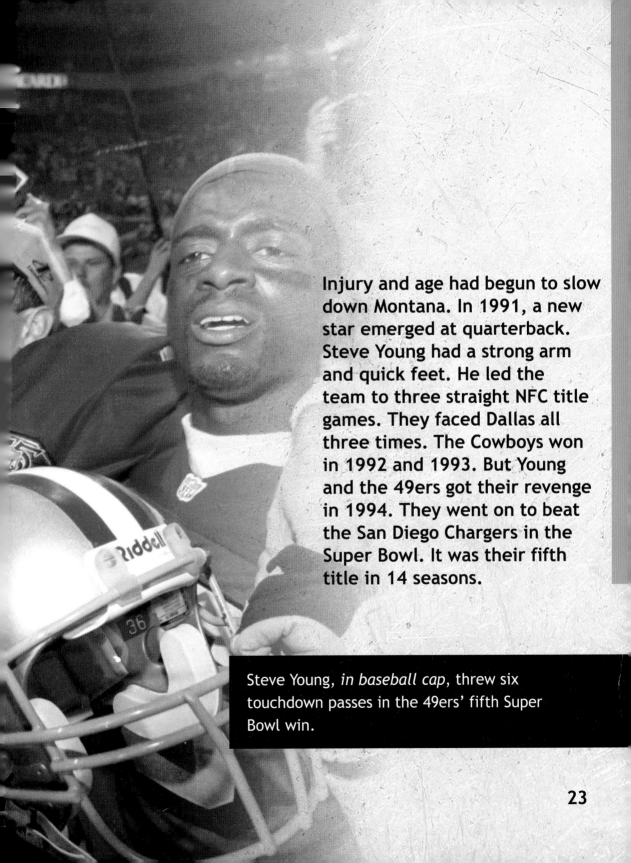

Injury and age had begun to slow down Montana. In 1991, a new star emerged at quarterback. Steve Young had a strong arm and quick feet. He led the team to three straight NFC title games. They faced Dallas all three times. The Cowboys won in 1992 and 1993. But Young and the 49ers got their revenge in 1994. They went on to beat the San Diego Chargers in the Super Bowl. It was their fifth title in 14 seasons.

Steve Young, *in baseball cap*, threw six touchdown passes in the 49ers' fifth Super Bowl win.

RETURN TO THE TOP

The 49ers fell on hard times in the 2000s. They were one of the league's worst teams. In 2011, they hired former Stanford University coach Jim Harbaugh.

Harbaugh quickly turned the team around. It started with defense. In Harbaugh's first season, they went from 16th in the NFL in points allowed to second. The 49ers went to the NFC Championship Game. The New York Giants beat them in overtime.

FAST FACT

From 1983 to 1998, the 49ers had 16 straight winning seasons.

Coach Jim Harbaugh, *left*, and quarterback Alex Smith led the 49ers to the NFC Championship Game in Harbaugh's first season.

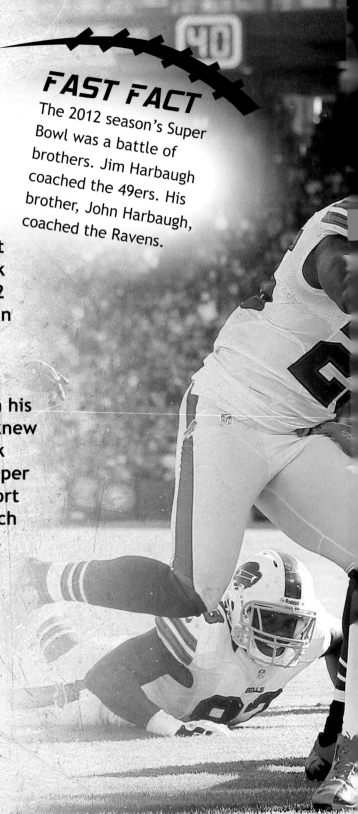

FAST FACT

The 2012 season's Super Bowl was a battle of brothers. Jim Harbaugh coached the 49ers. His brother, John Harbaugh, coached the Ravens.

The 49ers had another great season in 2012. Quarterback Alex Smith led them to a 6-2 start. Then Smith suffered an injury. Second-year passer Colin Kaepernick took over. Kaepernick was electric. He beat opposing defenses with his arm and his speed. No one knew how to stop him. Kaepernick led the 49ers back to the Super Bowl. However, they fell short of the end zone in a last-ditch drive. The Baltimore Ravens won 34-31.

Colin Kaepernick is known as a dual-threat quarterback for being able to throw and run effectively.

FAST FACT

Levi's Stadium is located in Santa Clara. It hosted the Super Bowl after the 2015 season.

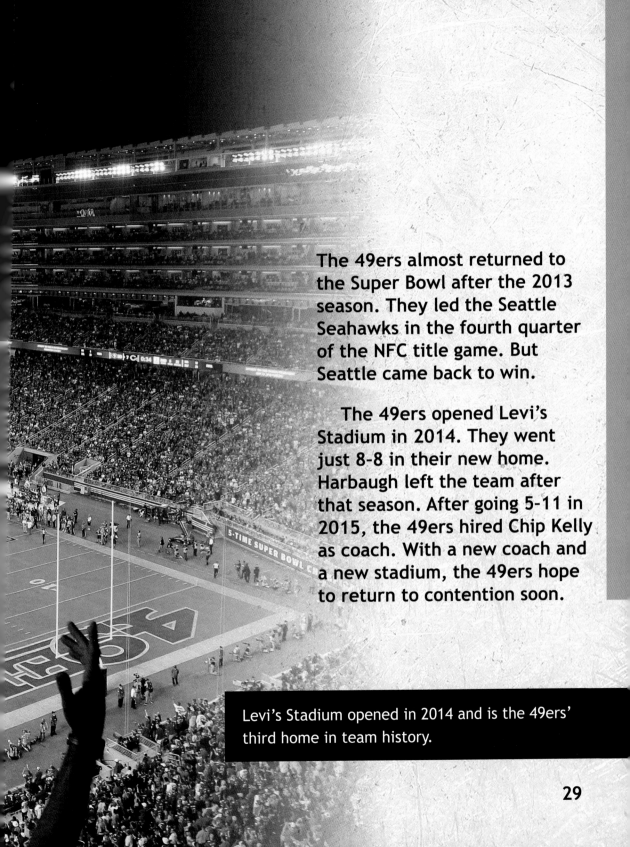

The 49ers almost returned to the Super Bowl after the 2013 season. They led the Seattle Seahawks in the fourth quarter of the NFC title game. But Seattle came back to win.

The 49ers opened Levi's Stadium in 2014. They went just 8-8 in their new home. Harbaugh left the team after that season. After going 5-11 in 2015, the 49ers hired Chip Kelly as coach. With a new coach and a new stadium, the 49ers hope to return to contention soon.

Levi's Stadium opened in 2014 and is the 49ers' third home in team history.

TIMELINE

1946
The 49ers are founded as part of the All-America Football Conference.

1950
The 49ers join the NFL. They go 3-9 in their first NFL season.

1968
The 49ers hire coach Dick Nolan.

1972
The 49ers win their third straight NFC West title.

1979
The 49ers hire coach Bill Walsh and draft quarterback Joe Montana.

1982
The 49ers finish the 1981 season with their first Super Bowl win on January 24.

1990
The 49ers finish the 1989 season with their fourth Super Bowl win in nine seasons on January 28.

1991
Steve Young takes over as the 49ers' starting quarterback.

1994
Jerry Rice sets the all-time NFL record for touchdowns.

1995
Young leads the 49ers to their fifth Super Bowl title on January 29.

2013
Quarterback Colin Kaepernick leads the 49ers to a 11-4-1 record and a Super Bowl appearance following the season.

GLOSSARY

DEFENSIVE BACK
A player who tries to keep receivers from catching passes.

DISBAND
To break up or stop functioning.

DIVISION
A group of teams that help form a league.

DYNASTY
A team that is very successful over a long period of time.

OVERTIME
An extra period or periods played in the event of a tie.

SNAP
The start of each play, when the center hikes the ball between his legs to a player behind him, usually the quarterback.

TIGHT END
An offensive player who sometimes catches passes but is also responsible for blocking.

WEST COAST OFFENSE
An offensive style that focuses on short, high-percentage passes.

INDEX

ABOUT THE AUTHOR

Matt Scheff is an artist and author living in Alaska. He enjoys mountain climbing, deep-sea fishing, and curling up with his two Siberian huskies to watch football.